The Butter Man

Elizabeth Alalou and Ali Alalou

Illustrated by Julie Klear Essakalli

ⓘ Charlesbridge

Every Saturday evening my baba makes a big plate of couscous for our family to eat for dinner. On Saturdays my mama is always at work, so I stay in the kitchen while Baba is getting the couscous ready.

Baba spends a very long time preparing the couscous. He uses a special pot that he brought all the way from Morocco in his suitcase. It's a big round pot with two parts. The bottom part is deep and wide. That's where he puts the meat and vegetables and spices. The top part is round and shallow and has holes in it. That is where he puts the couscous.

But the food cooks very slowly. As our house fills up with the fragrant, special Saturday-night smell, I can feel my tummy rumbling as I get hungrier and hungrier. But I don't bother asking Baba for a snack. He wants me to save my appetite.

One day when I was very hungry, I kept hanging around the kitchen, asking my *baba* for something to eat.

"No," he said. "You must wait for the couscous to be ready."

"But I'm staaarving!" I said.

Baba looked at me for a long minute, as if he were looking at me, but looking past me at the same time. That is the look he gets when he is thinking about *tamazirt*—that's what Baba calls the place where he comes from, far away in Morocco.

He didn't stop what he was doing. He kept right on working on the couscous, dumping the grains into a bowl, sprinkling them with water, and fluffing them with his fingers. Then Baba put the grains of couscous back into the pot to steam some more, and he took me on his knee. He said, "Nora, let me tell you the story of the butter man."

When I was a little boy, about your age, there was a time when my family didn't have much to eat. It hadn't rained in *tamazirt* for a very long time, and that meant that the crops didn't grow. Every year in the spring your *bahalou* harvested wheat, then took it to the threshing ground to thresh it, then to the miller to grind it into flour. Your *mahalou* would use that flour to make the grains of couscous, rolling it out in a flat basket with the palms of her hands. She also used the flour to make flat loaves of bread that she cooked on a smooth clay pot over the fire in our kitchen.

But that spring the wheat didn't grow thick and green; it was little and stunted and brown. That year the bags that came from the miller were not full, and there weren't many of them. After a while your *mahalou* started to make the plates of couscous smaller, and the loaves of bread smaller too.

Your *mahalou* used to make butter for us, and I loved the way, after I dipped my bread into it, it made a slippery feeling on the roof of my mouth. Then one day my father led our cow off to the *souk* to be sold. After the cow was gone, there was no more butter.

A few weeks after the cow was gone, your *bahalou* left too. He went across the mountains to look for work and left me home with your *mahalou*. The last sack of flour sat in the corner. Now it was only half full. After that, it seemed I was hungry all the time, as if there was a little mouse gnawing a hole in my insides. For a while, there was still a little bit of butter left, the spicy *oudi* that my mother had saved, but pretty soon there was only bread, and never enough bread, never enough to make me feel like my stomach was full.

One day I was very hungry, and when I looked at the piece of bread my mother gave me, I knew it wasn't big enough, especially not without a little butter to dip it in. It was hard and just a little bigger than the palm of my hand.

"Ma!" I said. "Don't you have just a little bit of butter for me?"

But I knew that the butter jar stood empty. I had run my fingers across the ridged bottom of the clay jar and licked them long after any taste of butter was gone.

"Ali," she said, "why don't you go outside and wait for the butter man? If he passes, ask for a little bit of butter to go with your bread."

I took my bread and ran outside, down
the steep hill by our house. I jumped over
the stream that had dried to just a trickle
and ran out to the dirt road. I climbed up
on a big rock that was nice and warmed
by the sun and waited for the butter man.

Lots of people came down that road. Sidi Lhou was walking back from the fields, a shovel thrown over his shoulder.

Fadma and Itto came back from the hills where they were gathering kindling. They had big piles of sticks strapped to their backs.

Moha and Lahcen, wearing woolen robes and plastic sandals, came up from the spring carrying sweating clay jugs of water slung over their backs. The big red truck carrying passengers from Boumalne came by, kicking up dust that made me spit and diesel fumes that carried the important air of faraway places.

"Did the butter man come?" Mahalou asked.

"No." I shook my head.

"What happened to your bread?" she asked.

"I ate it."

Mahalou smiled at me and shook her head.

"You should have waited for the butter man a little longer."

Every day after that, when Mahalou pressed a small
piece of bread into the palm of my hand, she said, "Run
along now, Ali. Run along and wait for the butter man."
Every day I ran down the hill to my perch to wait
for the butter man. And every day first I licked, then
I nibbled on the morsel of bread as I watched the people
of the village go by, forgetting for a while the gnawing
feeling in my stomach. And every day I returned empty-
handed. No more bread. No butter man.

One day the piece of bread my mother had given me was so small I could close my fingers all the way around it, and it was so hard that when bread was plenty, I would have tossed it to the cow to eat. I tried and tried to save it for the butter man, but that day I couldn't lick and I couldn't nibble. Two quick bites and the tiny piece of bread was already gone. There was nothing left. Nothing but the familiar creases on the palm of my hand.

I was looking down the empty road that disappeared around a corner and out of the valley with a terrible sinking feeling. What if today was the day that the butter man came? He would pass by with a sack bulging and oily with fresh sweet butter, and my hands would be empty with not a speck of bread left to dip into the sweet yellow mounds.

Just then, around the corner, came a figure, a pack slung over his back, and what looked like a sack in one of his hands. I scrambled down from my perch quick as a goat and ran down the road to greet him.

It was my father back from across the mountains! He had a sack of flour thrown over his back. In his other hand he held a straw basket with some carrots and onions and turnips nestled in the bottom, and, best of all, there was a piece of waxed paper folded up, which could mean only one thing—meat!

At home, it was a celebration! My father placed the fat new flour sack on the floor in the corner while he told us about the farm across the mountains where he had gone to work. I could hardly imagine the place he described—a farm with big flat fields that stretched into the distance and water that came not from the sky, but out of tin barrels on wheels.

While he talked, your *mahalou* set the big couscous pot on the metal ring over the fire. She chopped one onion and two carrots, then carefully set the rest of the vegetables aside for another day. That night we had the best couscous you can imagine, and I ate until my belly was as taut as the drums that are played in the *ahidous*.

I shifted in my baba's *lap to get* more comfortable, and I said to him, "But what about the butter man?"

"Well, Nora, I'm not sure if the butter man ever came by, but I know that the rain clouds did. Even in *tamazirt* it doesn't stay dusty and dry forever. In the months after Bahalou came back, the rain fell, then stopped, then fell again. At first it just sprinkled, dampening down the dust. Then it rained harder, and the rainwater started to soak in and soften the ground. By the time the next planting season came around, the stream near our house rose high on its banks, and the soil in the fields was a soft moist brown.

That spring, even though I had grown taller, the wheat in the fields grew as high as my head. We had plenty of flour and some left over. Your *bahalou* took the extras to the *souk* and used the money he earned to buy another cow. Then Mahalou started to make butter again, and the butter jar was full."

"That must've taken a very long time."

"Longer than the time it takes to prepare a couscous dinner, that's for sure," he said, patting me on the head.

Just then I heard my mama's key in the lock. Home from work! And my *baba* stood up and piled the fluffy couscous onto a big round platter and covered it with meat, carrots, turnips, onions, and all kinds of other delicious things.

"Dinner is served," he said, and placed the splendid dish on the table.

But even as we sat around the steaming platter with our spoons held high, we had to wait just one more minute.

Just long enough to say our blessing.

"Bismillah." In the name of God.

My mother and father and I all say it together, and the wait is over. We raise our spoons and dig in.

We eat and eat until we are full, and there is always some left to save for our lunch tomorrow.

Author's Note

The story that Ali tells Nora takes place in a village in the High Atlas Mountains of Morocco. The High Atlas Mountains span the central part of the country of Morocco, which is located in the northwest corner of Africa.

Berbers or Imazighen (ee-mah-ZEER-een) are the native people of North Africa. The language they speak is called Tamazight (ta-ma-ZEEK) or Berber. This language is spoken by an estimated 40 to 60 percent of all Moroccans, including almost all inhabitants of Morocco's mountainous regions. Most Berbers are Muslims, like Ali's family in the story. Many Berbers also speak Arabic, the other main language in Morocco.

In the High Atlas Mountains, people live in small villages that are clustered along river valleys. The primary occupation is farming. People grow wheat, barley, and potatoes, and they raise chickens, sheep, goats, and cows for their butter. Nowadays some villages have electricity and some roads are paved, but many still appear much as in Ali's story.

The mountain roads are difficult and often impassable in winter. Very few people have cars, so there are many peddlers who travel from village to village carrying their wares in packs on the backs of their mules. One day you might find a teapot repairman, or a traveling healer who treats illnesses. Another day a peddler might arrive who sells goods from the big town, like chewing gum and straight pins, or staple food items, like olive oil and butter. Since the peddlers walk from village to village, you never know exactly what day they might pass through.

Traditional Berbers wear distinctive clothing. The women and girls wear colorful striped blankets called *tahendirt* (ta-hen-DEERT) tied around their shoulders. The blankets are made out of wool because winters in the mountains are cold and snowy. The blankets have distinctive patterns of stripes that identify which tribe the women belong to. They also wear bright head scarves that are often embroidered with sequins. Men wear heavy woolen robes with hoods called *tajellebit* (tah-jah-LAH-bit) in the winter, or lighter cotton robes called *fokias* (foh-KEE-yaz) in the summer. Some men wear long bands of cloth wrapped around their head like a turban to protect them from the hot sun.

Everyone in the village has a lot of work to do. Men go to the fields to plow and plant. They harvest crops and take goods to the weekly *souk,* or market, to be sold. At the weekly *souk* you can also buy almost anything you need—anything from kerosene for lanterns to plastic buckets; from fragrant spices to fruits and vegetables brought in from neighboring towns. Women walk far into the mountains to gather sticks for kindling. They carry the sticks piled onto their backs in bundles almost as big as they are. They use these sticks to light their cooking fires. There are lots of jobs for children to do, but they still have time to play soccer and other games and attend the village school, where they learn to read and write Arabic, the official language in Morocco.

Glossary

Ahidous (AH-hee-doos): A traditional Berber line dance in which men play drums and both men and women sing and dance.

Baba (BA-ba): Father.

Bahalou (BA-ha-loo): Grandfather.

Bismillah (bee-smee-LAH): The traditional blessing Berbers say before a meal, meaning, "in the name of God."

Couscous (KOOS-koos): A traditional North African dish of pasta made from rolled semolina flour. The tiny grains of pasta are steamed in a large two-part pot similar to a vegetable steamer. Couscous is served on a large platter covered with meat and vegetables. It has become a popular and familiar dish all over the world.

Mahalou (MA-ha-loo): Grandmother.

Oudi (OO-dee): Butter. In Moroccan mountain villages many people do not have electricity for refrigerators. When butter is fresh, it tastes sweet, but to save it for longer periods of time, it is mixed with spices and packed into clay jars.

Souk (SOOK): A weekly Moroccan market where a wide range of goods, from fruits and vegetables to staples like sugar and oil, as well as household supplies, can all be found. In Berber villages, people usually go to the souk to both buy and sell.

Tamazirt (ta-ma-ZEER-t): The place where I come from, my country.

For Joey, Hannah, Nora, and Willis—E. A.

For Rabha Chaou—A. A.

For Moulay, Noor, and Zak—J. K. E.

Text copyright © 2008 by Elizabeth and Ali Alalou
Illustrations copyright © 2008 by Julie Klear Essakalli
All rights reserved, including the right of reproduction in whole or in part in any form. Charlesbridge and colophon are registered trademarks of Charlesbridge Publishing, Inc.

Published by Charlesbridge
85 Main Street
Watertown, MA 02472
(617) 926-0329
www.charlesbridge.com

Printed in China
(hc) 10 9 8 7 6 5 4 3 2 1

Illustrations done in gouache on Arches paper
Display type and text type set in Sabon
Designed by Susan Mallory Sherman

Library of Congress Cataloging-in-Publication Data
Alalou, Elizabeth.
  The Butter man / Elizabeth Alalou and Ali Alalou; illustrated by Julie Klear Essakalli.
    p. cm.
  Summary: While Nora waits for the couscous her father is cooking to be finished, he tells her a story about his youth in the High Atlas Mountains of Morocco. Includes author's note and glossary.
  ISBN 978-1-58089-127-1 (reinforced for library use)
  1. Morocco—Juvenile fiction. [1. Morocco—Fiction.]
I. Alalou, Ali. II. Essakalli, Julie Klear, ill. III. Title.
PZ7.A3149But 2008
[E]—dc22   2007002278

Color separations by Chroma Graphics, Singapore
Printed and bound by Regent Publishing Services
Production supervision by Brian G. Walker

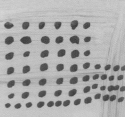

DATE DUE

GAYLORD	PRINTED IN U.S.A.